Charles Walter Palmer

The Weed

A Poem

Charles Walter Palmer

The Weed
A Poem

ISBN/EAN: 9783337158286

Printed in Europe, USA, Canada, Australia, Japan

Cover: Foto ©Andreas Hilbeck / pixelio.de

More available books at **www.hansebooks.com**

THE WEED:

A POEM.

BY

CHARLES WALTER PALMER.

'A cloud of smoke,
Wreathed, fragrant, from the pipe.'

THOMSON.

LONDON:

C. KEGAN PAUL & CO., 1 PATERNOSTER SQUARE.

1880.

PART THE FIRST.

PART THE FIRST.

ALL joys, all pleasures, known to mortal men
Have furnished topics to the poet's pen :
' Pleasures of Hope ' and ' Memory ' have been sung,
And even Melancholy's harp is strung ;
But none as yet of all the rhyming tribe
Have dared, my Theme, thy pleasures to describe.
Oh base ingratitude ! the scribbling crew,
When writhing underneath the sharp review,
All fly to thee for comfort, counsel, aid ;
'Tis at thy footstool all their woes are laid :
But if at last they make themselves a name,
Or raise a sign-post in the street of Fame,
They bow their judgments to a canting age,
Nor dare to give thy worth a single page ;
Hence I, unknown, unskilful, take the field
In thy behalf a maiden pen to wield ;
And humbly of the Muse assistance ask
As one unequal to the mighty task.

I dare not trouble all the tuneful Nine
Who on Parnassus dwell, for aid divine :
August Calliope but once an age
Fires Homer's song or Milton's awful page :
But once Melpomene's refulgent charms
A Shakspeare lure from sweet Thalia's arms ;
Till from their wild ecstatic loves are born
Othello's rage, wronged Timon's bitter scorn,
Macbeth's foul treason, Katharine's piteous woe,
False Richard's bloody rise and overthrow.
Not unto these dread queens of highest song
Dare I approach ; far off amid the throng
I loiter at the temple's outer gate,
And there the laughter-loving Muse await
Who with such wit adorned quaint Butler's rhyme,
That doggerel, in his hands, became sublime :
Who, long before, Parnassian heights forsook
And on a pilgrimage old Chaucer took,
What time that harbinger of dawning day
Dispelled the night of ages with his lay,
Thrilled England's heart-strings with a mighty song,
And to an infant nation gave a tongue.

Hush ! the bright goddess comes, she draweth nigh,
Mirth on her lips and mischief in her eye :
Earth dons her best the jocund dame to greet,

And strews the sward with flowers to kiss her feet :
Black Care, alarmed, in haste her coming flies ;
Mute Melancholy's victims, rescued, rise ;
Dulness and Folly fall, by Laughter slain ;
And Sorrow, smiling, half forgets her pain.
O thou who erst a Dryden's force supplied,
A Goldsmith's ease, my errant Fancy guide :
Make keen my vision hidden truths to spy,
My quiver with satiric shafts supply,
With flowing numbers round my halting verse,
My frail conceits to strength and beauty nurse.
Sage Clio ! thou Fame's blazoned scroll should'st bring,
And, clarion-voiced, a hero's praises sing,
Who paying homage due to all the Nine,
By life and letters both, was doubly thine ;
That duly honoured in my lay may be
The matchless Raleigh.   Of all courtiers, he
The best and wisest, spurns ignoble ease
To plough with daring keel the western seas,
And off Columbia's shores, in many a gale,
Doth hoist on high his bold adventurous sail.
First Briton he, great Weed, thy worth to own,
And make thy unregarded virtues known.
Far better had 'the rude imperious surge'
O'er a wild ocean howled his funeral dirge ;
Far better had some high tumultuous wave

Closed o'er his honoured, though untimely grave :
Not then his hapless lot had been to feel
The galling fetter or the headsman's steel.
The motley king who virtues found in Carr,
Who took a Villiers for his guiding star,
Could not discern true merit such as thine,
By Nature framed in court or camp to shine ;
But on a pretext frivolous and unjust,
His noblest subject in a dungeon thrust.
For thee, true heart, 'stone walls no prison made,
Nor iron bars a cage ;' e'en there displayed
To men unborn, thy genius took its flight,
And only stooped to set in endless night.
Thy mournful tale must not my page prolong,
Th' ethereal joys of smoking are my song :
Preached at in vain, maligned, and written down,
They laugh to scorn the puritanic frown ;
And spite of all that bigots do or say,
Have still maintained, and ever will, their sway.

Let bookworms still philosophy derive
From ancient sages, who did live and thrive
By launching systems down the sea of Time
When Rome was in her cradle, Greece her prime.
However grand each theory looks in print,
We find, when tried in practice, little in't.

If by philosophy we mean, to bear
With patience disappointment, pain and care ;
To suffer evil with undaunted soul ;
To keep our passions under calm control ;
Still unsubdued to see our hopes deflowered ;
To bear the shocks of fate with mind unsoured :
If this be Wisdom's true refinèd gold,
In Greek or Latin hawked about and sold,
Go ransack all, Pythagoras and Plato,
Yea, all from Zoroaster down to Cato ;
Search all that end in S or O at pleasure,
Whose uncouth names defy or rhyme or measure ;
An ounce of ' bird's eye ' and a pipe of clay
Will teach far more philosophy than they.
To treat of this requires an abler pen—
It well deserves the care of learned men,
And as for me, I have but little lore :
I was not reared where Cam and Isis pour
Their classic streams to fertilise the world,
Where Knowledge hath on high her flag unfurled.
O'er the wide ocean 'tis my lot to stray
Where mountain billows, rising, bar the way.
Not Learning here, but Seamanship avails
When Death himself, the mad tempestuous gales
Bestriding, shows his pale terrific form,
And hurtles on the demons of the storm.

My task 's an easier one ; full well I know
The tranquil happiness when upward go
The smoky cloudlets circling to the skies,
Till all our better feelings with them rise ;
While envy, hatred, discontent, retire
As if consumèd in the sacred fire
Which glows and sparkles in the heated bowl,
And pure enjoyment doth entrance the soul.
To sing of this, although the wayward Muse
With smile disdainful should her aid refuse,
The pipe itself would surely serve my turn,
When in its bowl the sacred ashes burn ;
And as I pace the quarter-deck alone
(The peaceful waters of the torrid zone
A thousand leagues around extending wide),
Its inspiration shall at least be tried.

O'er Ocean's bosom broods the shadowy night :
The crescent orb of Dian soon her height,
By starry hosts attended, will attain ;
And in her course the fleecy columns stain
With rose and amber ; though she may not try
With such resplendent hues to deck the sky
As fiery Phœbus doth around him shed
When first uprising from his ocean bed,
She hath a modest beauty, all her own,

As sweet to view, and chaster in its tone.
These happy regions rarely know the strife
Of jarring elements to mischief rife ;
But ever as the trade-wind briskly blows,
The silvery wavelets break beneath our bows,
And with such music thrill the midnight air,
Earth hath no harmony so sweet, so rare.
Like as the courser with long travel tired,
Nearing his stall, his energies new fired,
No more with hoof reluctant trails the ground,
But presses onward with a joyous bound,
And as each step the goal doth nearer bring
Makes the road echo back its iron ring,—
Our vessel, having weathered many a gale
Since first from Malabar we hoisted sail,
And struggled bravely 'gainst the adverse blast
Whose fury ofttimes threatened sail and mast,
With joy perceives her travail nearly o'er,
And hies her swiftly toward old England's shore.
England ! my home ! my country ! When my heart
Shall from its Ocean-Queen ungrieved depart,
Or cease when hailing thee at each return
With pure intensity of joy to burn,
Oh let thy briny vassals 'venge thy cause,
And him engulph that spurns at Nature's laws.

He who at home the daily task pursues,
And at its close, each happy eve, renews
The pleasures of the past one ; by the fire
To smoke and gossip with a genial sire ;
Or joins his sisters in a merry lay
When mirth and music while the hours away ;
Who sees before him, in her wonted chair,
A mother that with tender smile doth share
The happiness around her ; may not guess
The thoughts of him who for a mute caress,
A word, a loving look, must long in vain ;
And if, perchance, a falling tear should stain
His cheek when Nature thus asserts her reign,
Not less to manly courage be his claim :
A feeling heart doth not true manhood shame.

A tube we read of in an Eastern tale,
Whose magic powers were such, it would not fail
To bring at once before the gazer's eye
Whatever scene on earth he wished to spy.
'Twas by its aid the wandering princes saw
Their sire the sultan laying down the law
In full divan before a turbaned crowd,
While at each word the haughty vizier bowed.
Then at a wish, like a dissolving view,
The vision faded, and these lovers true

Essayed to raise the lady for whose sake
Did each his solitary journey take.
A tube as good, its magic power no less,
Of meerschaum made and amber, I possess ;
Its length about five inches (less or more),
With bowl elliptic and a narrow bore :
This, rightly used, will clear the inner sight,
And wing the fancy for its farthest flight.
But fill it with the *Weed* : apply a light ;—
And conjured by combustion, veiled in smoke,
The subtle genius whom these rites invoke
Its cloudy wrappings to the eye reveals,
And through the amber on its mission steals.
Yet how unlike th' intoxicating drug
Whose gross delights the swart Mongolian hug,
Which dulls the senses, stupefies the brain,
Brings idiotic torpor in its train ;
Whose votaries, revelling in fancied bliss,
Sink deeper in a bottomless abyss !
No dull besotting influences belong
To thee, ethereal essence of my song :
Though none of Nature's gifts will bear abuse,
No ill attends thy reasonable use.
Refreshed by thee, the mariner still can
With eagle eye the dim horizon scan ;
Still mark the trim of each wind-harassed sail ;

Still note the tokens of the coming gale ;
In the black cloud detect the lurking squall ;
Foresee all dangers, guard against them all :
Brightening his senses, dull from lack of sleep,
Thou aidest him his weary watch to keep.
Enough of this,—I rather here designed
To show thy wondrous action on the mind ;
How, freed by thee from earth's abhorred control,
It flashes unimpeded to its goal ;
Through the dull void of space at will to roam,
Or settle on the threshold of its home.
Thus I upsoaring on thy rising smoke,
My spirit from its earthy moorings broke,
Skim the vast arc of this terrestrial ball
Which parts me from my home at Elmshade Hall.

From yon old tower the evening bell hath tolled ;
The drowsy cattle slumber in the fold ;
No glowing sparks above the smithy rise ;
The smith's huge hammer unregarded lies.
Here, where the rustic dwellings shrouded lie
In darkness, unrelieved, against the sky,
The weary villager in cosy cot
Enjoys refreshing sleep, his cares forgot :
There, where the flickering taper's feeble light
Through the check curtain struggles into sight,

The son of toil, his children at his knee,
Joins in their sports and shares their simple glee.
The village merchant, licensed he to sell
Tea, coffee, and tobacco, snuff as well,
Weary of yawning expectation, goes,
With half-reluctant shrug, the shop to close.
That wondrous little shop ! how does it hold
The great variety of things there sold ?
Dry goods and groceries ; great coats and pills,
To keep the village warm and cure its ills ;
With all its patrons want, from shoes and socks
To patent medicines and children's frocks.
The shopman 's sure a wizard in disguise ;
Or else, coiled up beneath his counter, lies
Aladdin's genie, who of mighty works
Grown weary, here in snug retirement lurks,
And, tired of palace-building, takes his ease
In doling hardware, hosiery and cheese.
Yet not unchallenged is the silent sway
Of sloth-inspiring night ; across the way
The ale-house rings with shout and song and laugh
Of jovial souls who there good liquor quaff,
And hail with noisy mirth, o'er pots of beer,
The joyous time that comes but once a year.
Snug homesteads too, where sturdy yeomen dwell,
Farm-house and grange. show signs of life as well ;

The Weed.

For sons and daughters, scattered far and wide,
Now gather gladly round each old fireside ;
Friends parted long, with joy each other meet,
And in their happy homes the groups complete.
But stay : I came not here, Asmodeus-led,
To peer in stately hall or humble shed.
Although these visions rise before my sight,
No wayward humour guides my fancy's flight :
One sacred spot alone would I explore,
Nor tax my cloud-compelling spirit more.

O that I had the sweet descriptive skill
Which charmed the world in Goldsmith's 'angel quill,'
On this my page in vivid hues to trace,
And outline bold, the dear familiar place.
Vain wish ! though in my mind reflected clear
My home, its loved inhabitants appear,
Would I thereof a lasting impress take,
The airy shapes its ruffled disc forsake.
Thus, mirrored in a calm and silent mere,
The heavens above in duplicate appear ;
But, once disturbed, the waters rippling rise,
The surface ruffles and the semblance flies.
See yon old pile which scarce an arrow's flight
Back from the road, looms darkly on the right,
O'erhung with giant elms, majestic trees

That stand like mighty sentinels at ease,
And stretch their naked limbs athwart the sky
To ward off evil, should it venture nigh.
A relic it, of vanished greatness : when
Victorious Edward led his stalwart men
To wreak his anger on the foe in France,
Its knightly owner proudly bore a lance
Amongst the warrior train ; but how he fared,
What feats of arms achieved, what perils dared,
What toils encountered or what glory shared,
I know not : he himself were now unknown
Save for an effigy in sculptured stone,
Which clad in helm and mail, with ponderous blade
Cross-hilted, by his lady's side is laid
Within the church, to guard (a lasting trust)
The garnered handfuls of their common dust.

A relic, said I, of a glorious past?
When civil wars our smiling plains did blast,
And disaffection, turned to venomed hate,
With dire convulsions rent the unhappy state ;
Through yonder gate a gallant cavalier
Rode forth at honour's call to break a spear.
While yet he paused to take a parting look
At the sweet home he for his king forsook,
The swelling throat, set teeth, and heaving chest,

Betrayed the choking sob he scarce suppressed ;
The bloodshot eye, the slowly oozing tear,
Belied the smile he forced, his love to cheer :
Her kerchief fluttered forth a sad farewell—
He kissed his hand and turned—she swooning fell.
Then from yon hollow tree, to action stirred
By clash of arms, an owl, ill-omened bird,
Over the little troop a hovering flight
Essayed, but scared and blinded, from the light
Sought shelter in the nearest leafy shade,
And from his covert dismal hootings made.
The very watch-dog too with doleful howl
Joined in the bodings of the ominous fowl.
The village folk, assembled at the gate
To see their lord set out, with hope elate,
Had almost deemed his little band alone
Enough to keep the monarch on his throne ;
But when with superstitious awe they heard
The howling dog, the dismal hooting bird,
These signs of ill their spirits so depressed,
Each saddened face its rising fear expressed ;
And as the horsemen slowly rode away,
Left scarce the courage for a faint hooray.

Whenas to wisdom schooled, the chastened land
Had buried deep the slaughter-reeking brand,

Back to yon hall from dreary exile came
The heir to little but an honoured name ;
For where of late his father's house had stood,
He found a heap of stones and blackened wood ;
While of the acres that to it pertained,
By fine and forfeit wasted, few remained.
Part he recovered (all, be sure, he could)
But left untouched the ruins as they stood,
And at the Court to push his fortunes sought,
Or share his smiles whose battles he had fought.
I cannot sing, my muse is too precise,
The giddy round of folly and of vice
Which at that Cytherean court he shared,
And thus the remnant of his wealth impaired ;
But ere he yet had passed the flowery brink
Of ruin's yawning gulf where myriads sink,
Love, heaven-sent and pure, redemption wrought
Whereby he back to better things was brought.
How oft the weary traveller who strays
O'er Afric's desert plains, oppressed with rays
Of scorching splendour from the noon-day sun,
His water spent, his journey scarce begun,
With eye despairing scans the arid wild
To see the false mirage ; by which beguiled
He rushes on, when lo ! the grove, the stream,
Melt into air and vanish like a dream ;

And where he hoped his fevered lips to lave,
Hot burning sands replace the cooling wave.
But when at last the oasis is won,
With sparkling rill and shelter from the sun,
His choking thirst by copious draughts allayed,
He, happy, revels in the wished-for shade.
Should then the lying vision try its lure,
He inly laughs, from such deceit secure ;
No more in vain pursuits his vigour 's spent,
Safe in his Paradise he rests content.
Thus man, poor dupe, for happiness athirst,
With such mirage-like seemings ever cursed,
Is led astray by pleasures mean and vile,
The foul debauch or venal beauty's smile ;
But finding it in Love, unselfish, pure,
He scorns such shadows, of the substance sure.
'Twas Love, constraining Love, the spendthrift lured
From Pleasure's giddy haunts, his folly cured,
Who, wearying of Courts and courtly ways,
Resolved henceforth at home to spend his days.
With this intent he straight rebuilt the hall
(Not like the ancient one—his means were small),
There lived content, esteemed throughout the shire
A model Justice and a worthy Squire.
Not long his race outlived its wealth's decay,
The name with his successor passed away :

Now of their ownership no trace remains
Save diamond writings on the window panes,
And in the church some monumental stones
To mark their last retreat and hide their bones.

Though Time, old house, hath thee of much bereft,
Still at thy hearthstone Happiness is left ;
Still Hospitality attends thy gate
Right heartily, though with diminished state :
Though black with age, and of their beauty shorn,
Thy oak-lined chambers are not left forlorn,
For Woman's gentle feet about them roam,
And leave the prints which beautify a home.
Without, rude changes have thy seeming marred,
Thy lawn a paddock is, thy court a yard :
Thy pleasure-grounds, to fruitful gardens turned,
Sweet uses in adversity have learned ;
And though perchance less pleasing to the eye,
Rich compensation in their crops supply,
Save a small remnant, still to Flora spared,
'Twixt turf and flowers in due proportion shared.
Thy fount of stone, though with a Naiad graced,
Is choked and dry, the Naiad's form defaced ;
But still the spring wherein its waters fell
Is through the village deemed a healing well.
Though liveried grooms no more thy stalls frequent,

Whose lavish care, on mettled coursers spent,
Caparisoned for chase the willing steed,
Or battle at a monarch's direst need ;
While hob-nailed rustics haunt thy stables now,
And yoke the patient horses to the plough ;
Still ploughing is as noble in its place
As war's dread pomp or spirit-stirring chase ;
Nor are thy means as yet so much impaired
But for the hunt a sturdy hack is spared.

'Tis well for us that Time's capricious hand,
So oft stretched out to threaten or demand,
Repairs in part the breaches which it makes,
And freely gives while greedily it takes :
At yon old house his thefts are well repaid
In the home group now at its hearth arrayed.
Theirs the blest state which Jakeh's pious son
So ardently desired and doubtless won,
'Twixt poverty and riches placed content   .
With 'food convenient' unstinted sent,
Nor worn by want nor vainly puffed by wealth
To dull the soul or mar the body's health.

See first, erect and tall, of godlike mien,
With lofty front, commanding yet serene,
Amidst a small admiring circle stand

The chief, the father of the little band,
His youthful fire subdued, but not burnt out,
Though coming age hath sprent its snows about.
In counsel sage, by long experience taught :
Of flowing speech with wit and wisdom fraught :
With humour lurking in a latent smile :
Keen, shrewd and practical, but free from guile.
That facial outline, sharply cut and clear,
Would augur one, though just, to faults severe ;
But that in eye and lip we somewhat trace
That tempers justice with indulgent grace.
Nor doth he exercise such harsh control
As to rebellion drives the generous soul,
But wisely ready to resign the reins
To him whose ripening age discretion gains,
Can from a parent's honoured state descend,
And merge the father in the faithful friend.

Here Jubal see—the talent all his own,
To cull the sweets of harmony and tone.
By patient toil achieved, his art is such,
The sympathetic organ at his touch
(As o'er the ivory keys his fingers glide,
While pedals creak and stops obedient slide)
Leaps into life, a master's guidance feels,
Strains its huge lungs and bellows out in peals

Of soul-vibrating thunder: flute-like, clear,
The air in dulcet treble charms the ear ;
Hoarse brazen pipes their diapasons lend ;
The deep bass groans ; and all melodious blend.
His thirst for harmony, such its excess,
Rules him in all things, conduct, manner, dress.
In town, to business tuned, the shrewdest sense
Hath he of discount, profit, loss, expense :
Sedate and grave you meet him there and note
His spotless gloves and perfect-fitting coat ;
But in the country he affects the squire,
And roams about in easy loose attire,
With dog and gun. 'Tis said (but rumour lies)
That having, greatly to his own surprise,
Once shot a hare, he marched the village through,
To air his trophy in the public view.

Gruff honest Giles doth now our notice claim :
A herdsman he and husbandman of fame,
Whose practised eye needs scarce a beast survey
To note its value and its carcase weigh.
In tillage versed, 'tis his to use with skill
Plough, scuffle, harrow, seed-inserting drill ;
And, like a tyrant who by terror reigns,
Extort earth's treasures from its furrowed plains.
By nature wayward, irritable, wild,

He grew by smoking amiable and mild ;
And now is so transformed, who runs may read
Therefrom the virtues of the potent weed,
Whose fumes, extracted in the pipe's hot bowl.
So soothe the spirits and exalt the soul,
The temper mellows, ripens, and grows sweet
As doth green fruit in summer's kindly heat.

Next Dhaddai comes who follows honest gain
In busy mart, nor follows it in vain,
While music doth his idle hours amuse—
Or would, but that she flies as he pursues,
Though through the orchestra he runs apace
And with untiring zeal keeps up the chase.
Now in the organ's awful depths he dives,
Now o'er the vexed piano madly drives,
Through fiddle, harp, guitar, doth quickly range,
Then in the banjo seeks a soothing change.
Nothing above, nor aught beneath, his care,
Accordion, jew's-trump, bones his favour share,
Till, winding up the lasting long pursuit,
He pulls wry faces o'er a tortured flute.
As they who all attempt in nought excel
He plays all instruments and not one well ;
Kept true to one, despite himself—his tongue.
He can use that, and sings a famous song.

Last, but not least, the youngest one of all,
He Colin hight, a stripling fair and tall,
Hath David's comeliness and height of Saul :
Like David too, who Jesse's flocks did keep,
He rules his father's farm and tends his sheep ;
And like him still, his muse as yet unripe,
Sings sweetly shepherds' songs to oaten pipe.

Not without Scribbler were our group complete,
Who here by right prescriptive hath a seat.
Doomed through the day to uncongenial toil,
He to the Muses burns the midnight oil ;
The whilst, with hope deferred from year to year,
His chafing soul resents its sordid sphere ;
And like the genie in a jar confined,
Struggles in vain and can no egress find.
But Fortune's impress is no sacred seal,
Nor can it, ever, stubborn worth conceal :
Scribbler despite its weight shall have his day,
His bondage break and upward soar away.

Sing, if thou canst, the Mother next, O Muse,
Who doth through all the light and warmth diffuse
Of perfect love : whose sweet attractive force
Doth (as the sun's, harmonious in its course,
Each tributary orb,) her household guide,

All drawn to her and in her love allied.
Although my numbers sweetness lack and strength
To paint her glorious womanhood at length,
In Wisdom's ancient book the sacred page
Presents her counterpart,—the matron sage
Whose price is high above the rubies set,
Or gems which sparkle in the coronet :
Who eateth not in idleness her bread,
Nor, slothful, wastes the morning hours in bed :
But early sees her children's wants supplied,
Doth for her servants likewise well provide,
And stretching out her hand to aid the poor,
Turns not the beggar empty from her door.
'The law of kindness' on her lips enthroned,
Her voice is music, sweet and silver-toned ;
And if, when needful, for reproof employed.
Its pleasant chiding is of harshness void.
Though sharing in the general mirth the while,
Veiled sorrows dim the brightness of her smile :
Deep in her heart two missing ones she weeps,—
The one is far away, the other sleeps.
The wild Atlantic wave may one restore,
But one no earthly home shall welcome more.

With her the girls, who interchange apart
The gossip dearest to the female heart.

Those precious secrets too, in voices low,
Our ruder kind may guess, but never know ;
Though rosy blushes, titters half subdued,
Upon their merry converse oft intrude.
The sterner sex with arguments of weight
Behind a cloud discuss affairs of state,
Enjoy the weed and pass the flagon round,
While kindly satire, wit and mirth abound.
The rural franchise first ; but Hodge's vote
Is soon dismissed for things of greater note :
Home politics of small importance seem,
And pale before a more absorbing theme.
As some the Czar's integrity maintain,
Plan for his Tartar hordes the next campaign,
And wrest the Principalities away
From the lewd Mussulman's atrocious sway,
Others the despot's dark designs disclose,
Stript of its wool his grisly hide expose ;
And fear the devil in a robe of light
When Russia, armed, would freedom's battles fight.
But soon the girls their snug retreat find out,
Forth from their den the politicians rout,
Them captive leading merrily away,
Not half unwilling, Christmas games to play.

Now all are gathered round a roaring fire,

And there with wary answers try to tire
A grim persistent veteran, who goes
About in quest of money, food or clothes :
Collecting on his rounds, in lack of these,
Rings, lockets, penknives, handkerchiefs or keys ;
But should his begging prove of no avail,
Lulling suspicion with an artless tale,
A simple question as he turns to go
Draws from his victim an unconscious 'No.'
Having in time amassed a goodly prize,
Some blindfold volunteer the forfeits cries,
The laughter pealing in a perfect storm
As all, in turn, droll penances perform ;
While blushing maids, who much their fate deplore,
Receive a chaste salute behind the door.

Charades a merry party next engage,
Who from the room mark off a mimic stage ;
Then rummage dresses from the mouldering gloom
Of closets dark, and sack the lumber room,
Which dusty region, thoroughly explored,
With other treasures yields a rusty sword,
A huge horse pistol for a robber's belt,
With practicable hats of battered felt,
Which, broad of brim, may shade a parson's face,
Or, cocked and feathered. a bold brigand grace.

Scribbler with tattered gown, and whitened hair,
A miser is who hath a daughter fair ;
Young Colin acts the lover to the life
And woos the miser's daughter (Dhaddai's wife) ;
Jubal, the rival, ugly, rich, and old,
To whom the miser hath his daughter sold :
Of course the lover bears his lass away,
Defeats their vile intrigues and ends the play.
The rival troupe a tragic piece present
With sturdy rogues on midnight murder bent,
Whose plot a deadly combat doth afford
To find employment for the rusty sword.
Giles of a lonely inn the landlord plays,
Who oft the unsuspecting traveller slays ;
But doth to-night a very Tartar catch,
And in the hero Dhaddai finds his match.

Thus, fraught with joy and unalloyed delight,
Strides on apace the nimble-footed night,
Unfolding ere the noisy pastimes pall,
One quiet hour, the happiest deemed of all ;
When closing in a blithe unbroken ring
Around the hearth, whose glowing embers fling
Upon the time-stained walls fantastic shades,
A holy calm each kindred soul pervades.
The lights and shadows of a checkered past

The Weed.

O'er which sweet memories a halo cast,
Are now recalled ; while Hope rejoicing stays
To tinge the future with its brightest rays.
But when on one, in loving tones, they dwell
Who, absent long, is yet remembered well,
The mother turns her head to hide a tear,
The sire exclaims ' Were but Arion here ! '

Far hence Arion, on the billowy main,
Soothes his lone spirit with a cheering strain ;
And, like the Jews of old by Babylon's streams,
His home revisits in poetic dreams,
Who, were his worth as is his liking good,
Would sing as sweetly to a mightier flood.

My pipe is out—its airy visions fade :
The cloud-compelling sprite withdraws her aid :
On the last wreath of smoke she rides away
And leaves her tube a lifeless thing of clay,
As doth the soul its gross material frame
When death extinguishes the vital flame.
The weed, consumed, may to vile ashes turn,
But not its virtue : that no fire can burn ;
Nor doth its finer essence soar on high
Borne on the pungent fumes which heavenward fly.
Like as the dew and cool refreshing rain,

Dry up in part, but in effect remain
As scent in flowers, as verdure on the plain,
So doth the odorous leaf's ethereal part,
Effectually remain with brain and heart
(The spleen and dull despondency to cure)
As strength to do and courage to endure.
As I its cloudy magic oft employ
And, aided thus, sweet reveries enjoy,
Such high ennobling thoughts my soul possess
'Tis not in words their tenor to express ;
For how should language, to its utmost wrought,
In fixed expression clothe the errant thought?
Let him who can with geometric line
The vast immensity of space define ;
Who can eternity compute in years,
Or, looking upward, count the starry spheres ;
With oily pigments paint the sea and sky,
Or with a bucket bale the ocean dry,
Articulate the promptings of his mind,
His deeper thoughts in wordy shackles bind.

PART THE SECOND.

PART THE SECOND.

WHEN Saturn reigned—so poets sang of old—
Our new-born earth enjoyed an Age of Gold.
A Sun impartial through the zodiac strode,
And on each month an equal warmth bestowed :
A virgin soil, unfurrowed by the share,
Spontaneous tribute to its monarch bare :
Unchafed by storms, and lacking ships to spite,
Old Ocean slumbered in unconscious might :
No tempests o'er the pine-clad mountains blew,
Nor hail nor drenching rain, but balmy dew
Did in the vales the verdant sward renew.
The sheep unshorn, the fatted calf unslain,
The colt unbitted browsed the grassy plain.
Man, self-complete, without the tailor's aid,
In naked majesty walked undismayed ;
While lovely woman, modestly unclad,
At Nature's hand her sole adornment had :
So purely yet burned Love's celestial fire,

Her unveiled charms provoked no base desire.
Roofed by green boughs, the mossy bank their bed,
Housed without skill and without labour fed,
In blissful ignorance they lived a life
By vice unsullied, void of care or strife ;
Yet had their happiness this grave alloy,
The insipidity of changeless joy :
Free from the ills of which we now complain,
Their pleasures lacked the piquant sauce of pain :
The right was stunted that no wrong withstood,
And lack of evil neutralised their good.

As Jove's more vigorous hand the sceptre sways,
The universe a sterner law obeys.
Pent up in hollow caves no longer sleep
The angry gales, but scour the troubled deep,
Whose surges, breaking on the storm-lashed shore,
O'er the lone beach in muffled thunders roar.
Soon from the equinox the sun declines,
And varied seasons to the year assigns,
As suffering men by sharp experience learn
In blasts which freeze and rays which piercing burn.
By need impelled, the shrewder show their parts
In rude forestalments of the useful arts :
Of woven boughs, mud-lined, with straw thatched roof,
Some huts contrive, compact and weatherproof:

To clothing, some, inventive skill devote,
Who borrow from the ram his fleecy coat :
To labour, some, reluctant oxen break,
And with rude ploughs imperfect furrows make.
Some swain, inspired, converts the hollow reed
To tuneful pipe whence dulcet strains proceed ;
The youths, admiring, to its measures prance,
And thread with lissome maids the mazy dance.
Then Phœbus first unloosed the poet's tongue,
To sway the passions with a heaven-taught song.

In sweet simplicity and calm content,
'Midst rural joys, the Silver Age was spent ;
Till man, incited by his restless mind,
In knowledge grew, from virtue much declined,
Whose high achievements soon his hopes surpass,
Such wondrous progress marks the Age of Brass.
Now studious shepherds first the heavens explore,
Name the bright groups they scarce observed before,
Note where eccentric planets wandering shine,
And track the regal sun from sign to sign.
The tribes, their large increase too straitly bound,
Disperse abroad and rival nations found,
Which, grown corrupt, in murderous wars engage,
And merge the Brazen in an Iron Age.

Though some this legendary lore disdain,
As idle phantasy of poet's brain,
Who nought assume but rigid proof exact,
The Iron Age remains a stubborn fact:
An age of bloodshed, misery, and crime,
From where, in annals of remotest time,
Four petty kings o'er other five prevail,
In battle joined in Siddim's slimy vale,
To where grim Muscovite and ruthless Turk
Round Plevna carry on the bloody work.
Yet through its Stygian darkness many a star
Of high heroic virtue gleams afar ;
The torch of science too emits a ray
Of brightness shining toward the perfect day.

This age, its stubborn heroes, best belong
To her who taught a Homer's deathless song.
A milder, merrier Muse I here invoke,
To sing in fitting strains an Age of Smoke :
A glorious age which, scarce as yet begun,
Hath much already from hard Iron won,
And soon will all.   'Tis thus the orient sun,
When rising like a giant in his might
To quell the black-browed, grim, usurping night,
Doth on the mountain tops his foe surprise,
And first secure the regions next the skies ;

Then from the dismal shade, triumphant, gains
The dewy meadows and the open plains ;
The valleys next the radiant victor laves,
Last glens remote, deep rifts and gloomy caves.
So vast a theme, as touching all mankind,
I scarce can grasp : my song were best confined
To one more vigorous and gifted race
Which holds in arts and arms the highest place ;
The foremost too to burst the Iron yoke,
And taste the fruits of Freedom won in Smoke.

Ye sons of Odin, from whose sea-girt isle,
Secure 'gainst all assaults of force or guile,
Great Alfred's sceptre, in Victoria's hand,
Doth tropic isles and arctic wastes command ;
To whom vast continents dread homage pay ;
Whom swarthy millions reverently obey ;
Whose colonies are empires, boundless, free ;
Whose richly freighted ships throng every sea ;
Whose equal laws respect the poor man's right,
Yet curb the monarch and restrain his might :
Seek ye the sources whence such glories rise ?
Who views the subject with unjaundiced eyes,
But must perforce to this conclusion come,
That no mean factor in the mighty sum
Is Smoke ?

Long feudal tyranny prevailed,
And mail-clad peers the people's rights assailed ;
Long did the vassal 'neath his burden groan,
In vain demanding justice from the throne.
Kings in their high ambitious schemes engaged
With foreign wars their thirst for fame assuaged,
Gave to their suffering subjects small relief,
Nor dreamt of greatness but in others' grief.
Though some in sickly sentimental rhymes
Cry up the past, bewail the good old times,
Their eyes with chivalric pomp and splendour dazed,
Or Quixote-like with wild romances crazed,
How palpable the darkness of a night
Wherein the ideal champion of right
Was but an errant self-commissioned knight,
Whose doughty arm a rude redress supplied,
And wrought that justice which the State denied.
Yet such the glories of this warlike time,
We half forget its misery and crime ;
And never doth its star so brightly shine
As on the eve which heralds its decline,
When mighty Edward, from a ruined mill
Which hard by Cressy crowned the vine-clad hill,
With straining eyeballs scans the field below,
To mark the onset of his puissant foe.

'They come! they come! in serried files advance
The king, the peers, the chivalry of France.
The routed cross-bowmen are scattered, slain,
Charged by their horsemen, trampled to the plain.
My men at arms are drops to such a sea,
Must knaves and varlets then our bulwark be?
Varlets no more, but England's pride and boast:
They stand their ground: they face that countless host.
Back to the ear they draw the pliant bow,
And in its midst a storm of arrows throw.
St. George! the deadly shafts descend like hail,
They pierce the rider through his triple mail.
The very horses fall and choke the way,—
Shoot on, my merry archers, shoot and slay!
Great God, 'tis madness! can I trust my sight?
Is that young Edward's banner on the right?
False traitor, Warwick, thou shalt answer this
If aught befall my darling, there, amiss.
Turn back, rash boy, turn back,—if thou be lost
Too dearly bought were France at such a cost:
To win dread Charlemagne's imperial throne,
I would not meet thy mother, Ned, alone.
But hark that shout! 'tis "Victory" they cry—
The Frenchmen waver—see, they turn and fly.
The broken squadrons on their centre fall—
Charge home, Plantagenet!—they mingle all,—

The battle grows confused.   But swiftly thence
Yon horseman comes to cure this sharp suspense.
How fares my son?   What tidings of the fight?'
'The prince, my liege, yet lives ; but sad his plight
And great his peril : Warwick bid me speed
To crave thy succour : urgent is our need.
The foe, our numbers known, for very shame
Would on our heads requite his tarnished fame ;
While closing up to take us in the rear,
Doth France himself with large reserves appear.'
'Ha ! say'st thou so? to horse ! to horse ! but stay—'
Reflects the monarch, 'if I cast away
My last battalions thus, and still defeat
Ensue, with none to cover the retreat,
'Twere utter ruin : better far for me
To keep a passage open to the sea,
And take at least a remnant home from France.
My country first—the boy must take his chance.
Go tell my son this day to win his spurs :
Hence, not a man to his assistance stirs ;
Since he and his have nobly borne the toil,
Be theirs the glory and the victor's spoil.
Thou, to the front, where Arundel remains
Barred by the rout which chokes the narrow lanes ;
There bid my yeomanry a passage force
Through the blocked roads impassable for horse.

. But point the way ; cry, England's Hope is there !
The sturdy knaves will soon his hazard share.'

Right joyfully the stalwart yeomen hear
The welcome mandate : lustily they cheer,
Fling down their bows, their brawny muscles bare,
Then promptly toward the menaced prince repair ;
Like willow wands their ponderous axes sway,
And through the rabble cleave an uncouth way.
But sulphurous fumes in smoky columns rise,
Which hide the battle from the monarch's eyes :
Its din is silenced by a dreadful roar
Of fiery engines, never heard before,
(Dread novelty in war !) whose deafening boom
Foretells of feudal tyranny the doom ;
Since, armed with tubes which vomit death in smoke,
The meanest hind will spurn a tyrant's yoke,
Or if compelled to battle for his right,
On equal terms the mailed oppressor fight.

Yet heavier far than any forged at home,
Remain the spiritual bonds of Rome :
Those at the worst could but men's bodies bind,
These weigh the spirit down and chain the mind.
The Baron might his vassal's deeds control,
The Church would subjugate his very soul ;

Enforce a blind assent to all it taught ;
Proscribe the range of free unfettered thought ;
And who should dare against its rule rebel,
His body burn and doom his soul to hell.
This in His name at whose auspicious birth
' Goodwill to man ' was sung, and ' Peace on earth ' ;
Who, pitying suffering and assuaging grief,
Reproved, but never punished unbelief ;
And, modelled on the realm of God above,
Built up a Church of universal love.
How soon that Church, corroded with the rust
Of iron times, betrayed its sacred trust,
Replaced its Founder's lowliness with pride,
And for His simple truths vain rites supplied,
Stones for the living bread—yea, to His Word,
Traditions fond presumptuously preferred.
The fount of Truth, thus sullied at its source,
Grew stagnant soon and lost its vital force ;
While error reigned, and superstition blind,
Like a foul incubus, oppressed mankind.
Yet was there left a remnant, faithful, bold,
That dared unflinchingly the right uphold
Of man to ground his faith on reason's rules,
Despite the dictates of sophistic schools :
These sowed the seed : the crop did little good,
Until the soil was watered with their blood.

So vast the *vis inertiæ* of the State,
The power that moves it must itself be great ;
But, set astir, it hath resistless force
To crush what obstacles impede its course.
This motive power the Church itself supplied,
(Hot zeal to folly sure is near allied !)
Which with its foes against itself took part,
And roused the nation's judgment through its heart.
Soon England, sickening in a lurid glare
Of persecuting flames, its wholesome air
Tainted with shrivelled flesh and calcined bones
Of charred humanity, with horror groans
To see the Smoke from blazing faggots rise,
Where martyred innocence in torment dies.
In vain a bigot queen her ermine stains
With blood of slaughtered saints, the Truth remains :
Though malice wounds and ignorance assails,
It all endures and in the end prevails.
Her ruthless reign, with dungeon, rack, and stake,
Did but the lingering attachment break
The nation for its ancient church retained,
And for the new an earnest hearing gained,
Which in due time a full deliverance wrought,
And freed from papal ban the world of Thought.

O Liberty ! thou priceless gift of God,

Whom long our fathers sought, and seeking trod
In rugged paths with weary wounded feet :
With whom, the mountaineer in rude retreat
Esteems his hard-earned bitter morsel sweet :
Without whom, plenty and luxurious ease
But yield satiety and fail to please :
How like the bow of promise, when pursued
Thou dost thy eager votaries elude,
Who, toiling on, to strength and virtue rise,
And what they dearly purchase, dearly prize.
Our sires, from vassalage and serfdom freed,
Pursue thee still with unabated speed,
But bursting soon the bars of prisoned Thought,
Supinely deem the final victory fought ;
And, tyranny of priest and peer put down,
Repose beneath a mightier one—the Crown,
Whereto, the nobles awed, the Church subdued,
Enlarged dominion speedily accrued.

Bluff Henry's ruthless violence, allied
To Cromwell's craft and Wolsey's soaring pride,
Such breaches in the constitution wrought,
That parliament became a thing of nought,
Which, though it held its formal sessions still,
But gave expression to the royal will ;
And what of 'thoroughness' their system lacked

Queen Bess supplied, with her unequalled tact.
That great Queen's nobler attributes conceal
Grave ills which undermined the public weal ;
Though doubtless patriotic, wise, and just,
And worthy of a loyal people's trust,
Her bold assumption of despotic sway
(Perhaps not without its uses in her day)
Might soon a dangerous precedent create
Nor, haply, rouse resistance till too late.
Thank God ! a constitution yet remained
Whose empty forms a spark of life retained,
Which burst at last into a mighty flame,
And thrilled with eager life its sluggish frame,
When once again the potent voice was heard
Of parliament, to sudden action stirred ;
Which, waking from a long inglorious trance,
Did stubbornly long dormant claims advance,
And though it much the painful task deplored,
Coerced the Queen it loyally adored.

Ye wise ones, who the secret springs detect
Of great events, and of each known effect
(So throughly versed in Fate's mysterious laws)
Trace back the hidden predisposing cause,
Say whence this ardent public spirit rose
Which, rousing the nation from inert repose,

Forced it its utmost energies to strain
In Freedom's cause ; and not alone to gain
Itself true liberty with law combined
(Wherein her sole security we find),
But in her bright array to lead the van
And teach the art of government to man.
All dumb and voiceless ?   Then the task be mine,
By Clio aided and her torch divine,
To read the riddle : though succeeding times
Mock my crude verses, ridicule my rhymes,
For this discovery alone I claim
A niche obscure in the bright fane of Fame.

Illustrious Raleigh, whose prophetic ken
Outstripped the bounded views of meaner men,
With politician's brain and poet's sight
The secret pierced of England's future might ;
And of her vast colonial empire dreamed
As yet unborn, wherein he wisely deemed
(Like Samson's cherished locks, of strength divine
At once the inward source and outward sign),
The destined crown of Britain's glory lay,
Who in the noontide splendour of her sway
Should far outshine the waning star of Spain,
And o'er the deep without a rival reign.
No idle dreamer he, but nobly sought

To give in form substantial, soaring thought
A prompt expression ; fitted out a fleet,
Freighted and armed, with needful stores replete ;
And lavish both of energy and gold,
Luring by wild adventurous dreams the bold,
The indigent by hope of plenteous gain,
Manned and dispatched it o'er the untravelled main
(Had fortune but the undertaking blest),
To plant an infant Britain in the west.
He failed—yet be his glory none the less,
Man can but merit, not ensure success—
If that be failure justly deemed indeed,
Which cleared the way for others to succeed,
And gathered as its own immediate prize
The choicest gift a teeming earth supplies.
Not Drake, who made a spheric ocean feel
The wake continuous of a circling keel ;
Who with scant crew, some hundreds at the most,
Sacked for a thousand leagues a guarded coast ;
Who dared the unknown trackless void assay
Which from the Andes stretched to far Cathay ;
And anchoring in the Thames his canvas furled
Above the treasures of a ransacked world :
Not Drake himself, in all his booty, bore
Aught half so precious from Peruvian shore,
Though bars and massy ingots lined his hold,

His ballast silver and his lading gold.
Yet 'twas no gem from subterranean cave,
No pearl of price, reluctant ocean gave,
No gorgeous fabric wrought in Indian loom,
No Javan spice, no Arabic perfume ;
But what them all in worth did far exceed—
' Divine Tobacco,' estimable weed !

When, Ocean's briny limits safely passed,
Our eager colonists their anchors cast
Off Roanoke, the promised land in sight,
Hailing its shores with rapturous delight,
They disembarked in haste ; and on the strand,
With all their poor resources could command
Of pomp and show, did in their monarch's name
Both continent and isles adjacent claim.
Then, with exulting shouts that rent the sky,
The royal banner hoisted up on high ;
Whose silken folds did scarce th' ascent begin,
Than kettle-drums' reverberating din,
Sonorous strains from trumpets brazen throats,
Loud clash of cymbals and the fife's shrill notes,
Awoke the thunders of saluting ships
In roars responsive from their iron lips.

Well might the dusky children of the wood,

Who mute admirers of the pageant stood,
Awed with the dreadful cannons' loud alarms,
The bearded faces, and the burnished arms,
Deem their strange visitants some heavenly race
That with its presence deigned the earth to grace.
Soon chief and warriors, scantily arrayed
In paint and feathers, leave the leafy shade
The godlike strangers' friendship to implore,
And bid them welcome to the red-man's shore.
Taught by their gestures and expressive signs,
The pale-faced chief their purpose soon divines,
Accepts their amity, and nothing loth,
Confirms the friendly compact with an oath.
The sachem gladly from his belt unloosed
The calumet, and fragrant leaves produced
Wherewith he filled the bowl; then fire applied,
And with *a smoke* the treaty ratified.
The white men much the novel sight admire,
To see the chief inhaling smoke and fire;
Whose wonder doth beyond all bounds increase,
When to their leader he the ' Pipe of Peace '
Presents, and by his gestures seems to ask
Him too, to follow in the dreadful task.

Thereto by curiosity inclined
And courtesy which sways the generous mind,

E

Therefrom by fear and timid doubts deterred,
Contending passions long his bosom stirred,
Whereat his face alternate flushed and paled ;
At last the nobler sentiment prevailed :
Resolved, at least, the odorous smoke to taste,
The pipe between his lips he firmly placed.
Scarce knowing if the fumes offend or please,
Clearing his nostrils with a vigorous sneeze,
Another and another whiff he tries
Till tears of anguish glisten in his eyes ;
But soon, alas ! such qualms upon him steal
As landsmen in a storm-tossed vessel feel ;
A ghastly grin his mouth, contorted, takes ;
The curdling blood his livid front forsakes ;
For water like a maniac he cries
And, sickening, feels his gorge, convulsive, rise ;
Thrusts the dread tube into his comrade's hand,
Avoids the scene and wallows on the strand.

That comrade, Herriot, wiser than the rest,
A sage's philosophic soul possessed,
A stronger stomach too, with busy brain
By observation trained new lore to gain.
He, noting of this smoke the dire effects,
Admires the strange phenomenon ; reflects
That what on Folly wrought such grievous harm

To Wisdom might supply a healing balm ;
Of strong medicinal virtue deems the weed
From whose rash use such sufferings proceed ;
And on himself resolves its power to try,
To live for Science or for Science die.
Such zeal as this the gifted Pliny urged
When fell Vesuvius its entrails purged
Of flaming horrors from a nether world,
And at doomed Pompeii destruction hurled.

Rejoice, O happy Muse ! to celebrate
A Pliny's courage here without his fate ;
And you, fair maids, whose hearts with pity melt
Beforehand, at the dreadful pangs he felt,
Dry your dimmed eyes, your wasted tears recall,
He smoked away—and felt no pangs at all.
He, Herriot, smoked that pipe, and smoked it out,
Yet was his stomach no wise put about ;
But as he smoked a sweet quiescence stole
Through every nerve and fibre to his soul,
Now raised above the paltry cares of earth
And all the vain desires which give them birth.

I sing not here, since sage historians tell,
What dire mishaps the exiled band befell ;
How sickness, famine, war, upon them preyed,

Waiting for promised succours long delayed,
Till hope deferred expiring, courage failed,
And such despair the homesick crew assailed,
With heavy hearts they re-embarked and sailed.

But say, ye powers that prompt heroic deeds,
From whom in undeserved distress proceeds
Our dearest consolation, what relief
Or solace found ye for the bitter grief
Which in the great projector's bosom burned
As homeward thus the empty fleet returned,
And he the sad disastrous issue learned
Of his great expectations? At his need
He solace found and comfort in the Weed.
For when the wanderers did on him wait,
The story of their failure to relate,
And strange adventures on that distant shore,
Pipes and Tobacco Herriot with him bore ;
Who rightly deemed their pleasurable use
Would best his patron's buoyant spirit loose
From sorrow's sullen sway, and strength impart
To bear his crosses with a manly heart.

'Twere needless, now that millions daily find
A balm, in smoking, to the harassed mind,
Wherewith both stricken soul and wearied brain

Renew their strength, their normal tone regain,
In Raleigh's case minutely to rehearse
A weed-wrought cure from disappointment's curse :
How, smarting sore 'neath shrewd Misfortune's stroke,
He proved the healing virtue of *a smoke* ;
And felt what weight of care his spirit bowed
Dissolve and mingle with the filmy cloud.
His lofty soul, thus cheered, refused to deem
The final issue of its glorious scheme
Involved in one miscarriage : that, his mind
Cleared and refreshed, he to th' effect assigned
Of accident or adverse Fortune's ban,
And not essential error of the plan ;
Nor judged the cost and labour thrown away
Which brought Tobacco to the light of day.

Not long content in solitude to taste
Ethereal joys, or on himself to waste
What Nature for the common good of man
Had bounteously bestowed, he straight began
To teach amongst his friends (soon scholars ripe)
The kindly pleasures of the social pipe,
Who with such zeal the sweet contagion spread
That through the kingdom it like wildfire sped :
For though the hoary sage who would impart
New principles of wisdom, science, art,

Mechanic skill, or philosophic lore,
Oft finds a giddy world his pains ignore ;
The man who would a novel pleasure teach
Will never long without a hearing preach ;
Nay more, the listening throng will inly yearn
To put in present practice all they learn.

Imagine ye, who all your lives have been
Familiar with the Weed, and ever seen
Mankind at large its soothing influence own ;
Who have, as 'twere, from youth to manhood grown
Wrapt in its fumes : imagine, if you can,
Society ere *Smoking* first began ;
Thus may ye best conceive the change it wrought
In manners, conduct, conversation, thought ;
See how its introduction caused at once
A moral revolution.   Where's the dunce,
Nurtured in ignorance, in dulness bred,
In folly steeped, by prejudice misled,
Who dares dispute the truths I here advance,
Or fails to see them at a single glance?
If such, alas ! there be, for him in vain
Hath been of wholesome birch the quickening pain ;
Or else Athena's beadle-scouts have lacked
The rigour needful to enforce the Act,
And left him idly wandering, free as air,

Far from the school-board's mild paternal care.
Yet such, if such there be, can scarce refuse
To listen to the mild persuasive muse,
Who after Truth in flowery paths would stray,
And, loitering, pluck sweet posies by the way ;
But all thus lost in method gains in force,
Should Reason rule her wild erratic course.

When Raleigh's ships the herb Nicotian brought,
Our sires were men of action, not of thought.
There was deep thinking then, right reason too,
But both peculiar to the learned few.
The grosser herd, who spent in toil the day,
Relaxed, at eve, in rude and boisterous play,
Sports often of a coarse debasing kind
More apt to lower than elevate the mind.
Oh what a grand resource, great Weed, to these
Thy pleasures, which to meditative ease
The dull vacuity of idlesse change,
Whether in mud-walled cot or moated grange ;
And with like zest enforced inaction crown
In solitude remote or busy town,
As through the dreary long December night,
Cosily basking in a ruddy light
Of blazing logs, beneath thine influence bland
The smoker feels his freshened soul expand ;

Now dares aloft on Fancy's pinions soar,
Now deeply thinks who never thought before.
If thus thy fumes, with inspiration fraught,
The art of thinking in retirement taught,
'Twas thine no less the sparks of truth to fan
Which friction oft struck out 'twixt man and man ;
Of conversation, thine to raise the tone,
Too oft degraded to a senseless drone.
The worthy souls who met by tavern fire
To hold discourse or current news inquire,
Kept up, to banish dulness, deadly sin,
A ceaseless clamour and incessant din ;
And since 'tis given but to a favoured few
To talk unsparingly and wisely too,
What wit they had and wisdom oft were drowned
In floods of gabble and unmeaning sound.
'Twas thine to substitute for idle speech
A silence not unsocial : thine to teach
How fewer words, by deeper thought refined,
Could more delight and stimulate the mind ;
And since a common topic of debate
With smokers is the business of the State,
Soon, nursed by thee and cradled in thy smoke,
Public Opinion in its strength awoke,
Which, mightier far than either pen or sword,
The failing balance politic restored.

Of old, when tyrant kings misruled the land,
Our stalwart sires unsheathed the righteous brand,
With bow and bill their stubborn lord withstood,
And drowned oppression in a sea of blood ;
But armed rebellion, devastating war,
The grim ally true patriots most abhor,
Might not, dread fiend, be summoned up at will
With fire and sword to cure each trifling ill :
Nay, rather than its fatal aid implore,
Men oft their grievances in silence bore ;
While roused Opinion could with jealous eye
E'en in its germ the coming evil spy,
When straightway, in the Senate, at its frown
That steady opposition to the Crown
Upsprung, which with a surgeon's dainty hand
Could both the caustic and the knife command,
And every plague spot from the commonweal
At no great risk eradicate or heal.

Though some who reason not, but blindly guess,
Derive Opinion from its slave, the Press,
Small skill it needs such nonsense to refute.
While yet the Press on State affairs was mute,
Opinion's voice the great Eliza cowed,
And so her proud imperious spirit bowed,
That she, the haughtiest Tudor of them all,

When pressed her wrongful patents to recall,
Did the abhorred monopolies withdraw,
And yield a tardy homage to the law.

The twice-crowned ass who, born beyond the Tweed,
Did to a fairer heritage succeed,
Presumptuous fool, its liberties assailed,
And hoped to prosper where the Tudor failed !
Yet would his wary subjects not resign
Their grand inheritance to 'right divine ;'
But strove, throughout his weak inglorious reign,
A fuller freedom, step by step, to gain.
And well the crafty pettifogger knew
From whence its strength the Opposition drew
Which dared in parliament confront his wrath,
And with such sharp restraints hedged in his path
That, autocrat in heart, he ever lacked
The kingly courage to be one in act.
Hence might he well, with mean vindictive spite,
The blameless Weed maliciously indict,
Till all his pent-up venom burst at last
In that foul libel 'clept the 'Counterblast.'

Leave we this driveller for his erring son,
Unhappy Charles, by vicious lore undone.
His father's precepts warped his infant mind ;

And as the twig was bent, the tree inclined.
Deeming kings gods, and subjects common clay,
Who must a monarch's lightest whim obey ;
Fawned on by flatterers for selfish ends,
And them preferring to plain-dealing friends :
His native worth by evil counsels spoiled ;
And early with his parliament embroiled—
Not wisely firm, but obstinately bold,
He scorned to be by its advice controlled,
Broke from its guidance in an evil hour,
And grasped the reins of arbitrary power.
But Public Opinion, thus defied, alone
Soon proved itself far mightier than the throne ;
Constrained, ere long, the humbled king to yield
Without the horrors of the tented field ;
And from him, vanquished, wrung a forced consent
To all the just demands of parliament.
Passive resistance, vigilant and stout,
In twelve short years had fairly starved him out.
Too late ! the factious Commons in their turn,
Flushed with success, for full dominion yearn,
Forcing their lawless king the sword to draw
And straight become the champion of the law.
But from his fall (grim irony of Fate !)
Not from his triumph, they their bondage date ;

And from their monarch's lawful sceptre free,
Before a great usurper bow the knee.

Thou master spirit of this troubled time,
Portentous man of piety—and crime !
But half a hypocrite, as much a saint,
What mind can measure thee, what hand can paint?
For empire born, that thou didst it acquire
Who most condemns thee must as much admire.
That for it thou didst pawn thine honour's gem,
Who most admires, alas ! must more condemn.
Hadst thou, content thy duty to discharge,
But listened to the bard's prophetic charge,
And *flung away ambition*, striven to heal
The nation's wounds, and sought the public weal,
A ' Cromwell guiltless of his country's blood '
Had aye on Fame's sublimest summit stood.
But, greatly tempted, thou didst greatly fall,
And to a throne through blackest treason crawl ;
Compassed thy monarch's end ; abused thy trust ;
So trailed thy tainted honour in the dust,
That, though great virtues thy great crimes oppose,
Not all Carlyle's grotesque bombastic prose,
Waller's sweet strain, or Dryden's flattering rhyme,
Not even grand old Milton's verse sublime,

Can from thy brow efface the brand of Cain,
Cleanse from thy bloody hands the damning stain.

O bitter degradation, erst unknown,
An iron sceptre and a despot's throne,
Where violence, in arms, by terror reigned,
And trampled right and liberty enchained :
Accursed be he who, to her foul disgrace,
Such yoke imposed on Albion's haughty race !
Yet was the harsh dominion of the sword
Their just reward, who liberty ignored
When in their grasp, chose anarchy instead,
And loosing substance, for a shadow bled.
Thus what opinion gloriously begun,
By arms continued, was by arms undone :
The lawless force which lent its traitorous aid,
The sacred cause it undertook, betrayed.

Nations, like men, experience seldom gain
Save by a sad apprenticeship of pain,
Thrice happy if, however dearly bought,
Calamity be with instruction fraught.
England her losses thus to profit turned,
And too much wisdom from her sufferings learned
To be again deluded with a show
Of freedom based on order's overthrow ;

Learned too, when forced again 'gainst wrong to fight
To trust those flawless weapons, Truth and Right.
Taught patience in affliction's bitter school,
She bore awhile the second James's rule :
Still loyal to his person, though she saw
His high prerogative bear down the law ;
Beheld the madman, unresisting still,
With statutes of the realm dispense at will ;
Till by her strained forbearance much misled
(As base submission sprung from slavish dread)
He shamelessly his sacred trust betrayed,
And impious hands upon her altar laid—
To fall, like Uzza, 'neath the avenging rod,
Who touched presumptuously the ark of God.

But though at this her wrath, long smothered, blazed.
Her moderation all the world amazed,
Which in her orderly rebellion saw
Revolt controlled by precedent and law.
No traitor clamoured for his monarch's head,
No Laud, no Strafford on the scaffold bled ;
For by a bloodless revolution freed,
She but her tyrant's banishment decreed ;
Nor dragged, this time, in hideous ruin down
Church, constitution, parliament and crown ;
But rather did the nicest care employ

To perfect that we to this day enjoy :
. A goodly pile on freedom broadly based,
Each atom, rank on rank, in order placed,
Whose sloping sides by due gradation rise,
Extend on earth and taper toward the skies,
To where (a summit of a single stone)
The monarch sits in awful state alone.
'Twas with like art old architects designed
Those granite piles we still in Egypt find,
Which, ruin-proof, preserve their ancient state,
Firm as a rock, immutable as fate.
Though domes collapse and massive walls decay,
Though arches crumble bit by bit away,
Though turrets quake and lofty columns fall,
The eternal pyramid outlasts them all.
Though round its base resistless tempests rage,
It stands in fixed repose from age to age ;
Confronts unhurt the blasting fell simoom,
And mocks at hoary Time's destructive broom.

Thus from a novel point of view I've scanned
The thrilling story of my native land ;
And half in earnest, half perhaps in joke,
Perused its records through a cloud of smoke ;
Yet know, he Clio's spirit best divines
Who reads her manuscript between the lines,

Notes not alone what chroniclers have writ,
But studying too the matter they omit,
Doth from his soul a pedant's trammels cast,
And in his fancy reconstruct the past.

And not in our enfranchisement alone
The progress of the Age of Smoke is shown :
The crafts whereby our toiling millions thrive,
Our wealth, our greatness too, we thence derive :
Our manufactures, shipping, mining, trade,
All stand indebted to its fostering aid.
Before the world its mighty impulse felt,
Labour right niggardly her products dealt :
Spindle and distaff, diligently plied,
But inch by inch the slender yarn supplied :
The weaver, o'er his engine stooping low,
Could but a solitary shuttle throw,
Both hands employed and treadling feet as well
To furnish forth of cloth a paltry ell.
He too whose mighty arm and skilful hand
Forged the hind's coulter or the warrior's brand,
As 'neath his clanging stroke the anvil rung
With painful toil his ponderous hammer swung ;
And could uneath brute force sufficient find
To mould the stubborn metal to his mind.

No useful art, no industry, no trade
Could fairly flourish while it lacked the aid
Of that all-potent sprite an Age of Smoke
Did from the earth's capacious womb evoke.
But where his fanes, colossal chimneys, rise
To smirch with Stygian fumes the azure skies,
At once unnumbered spindles deftly twine
By tons the staple into filmy line ;
While shuttles, not by aching fingers cast,
Athwart the opening warps in thousands passed,
Through tireless automatic looms defile
Which turn out woven fabrics by the mile.
The iron-worker's sledge too, left behind,
Or to the rustic shoeing forge consigned,
Hath at the foundry been supplanted quite
By ton-great hammers of exceeding might
(Whereat old Vulcan's self would stand aghast,
E'en Thor admit his mighty maul surpassed),
Beneath whose crushing weight and ceaseless play
The sternest metal yields like plastic clay.

Though in our handicrafts he serves us well,
The genius of the age doth more excel
In locomotion : his the magic might
Which spurs the iron courser on his flight :
That roaring monster whose terrific pace

Annuls the old restraints of time and space,
To whirl mankind at will from place to place :
Nor can earth's utmost verge his march restrain
Who makes a highway of the trackless main.

When man first dared to trust himself afloat
On raft, canoe, or rudely fashioned boat,
He in his hand the simple paddle held,
And by its sweep his tiny craft propelled.
Soon more expert, he learned to skirt the shore
In nobler vessels, toiling at the oar.
When to the sea inured, and bolder grown,
He longed to scour the deep from zone to zone,
Finding the weary oar no more avail,
He rigged the mast and spread the swelling sail.
But here invention paused—whole centuries past
And let him still depend on sail and mast ;
Still let him woo the wind's capricious aid,
By tempests hurried or by calms delayed ;
Still let him, forced by adverse gales to tack,
Describe a devious and uncertain track.

'Twas for this age deferred, this Smoky Age,
Successfully the problem to engage ;
Since Fate for it the building did reserve
Of ships that for no wind, no current, swerve.

When fiery furnaces within them gleam,
And smoky pennons high abaft them stream,
The tyrant waves, oppressed, submissive flow
To bridge for them th' unfathomed depths below.
And oh, how brightly in its annals shine,
Cunard, the records of thy matchless Line !
That joining link betwixt two hemispheres
Which o'er the baffled deep for forty years
Did passengers and mails, unceasing, bear,
Nor any lost committed to its care.

Not that the seaman's cunning aye avails
To balk the fury of Atlantic gales.
As when the pard, or wolf with hunger bold,
Attempts by night the watched and guarded fold,
And powerless to molest the silly sheep,
Doth, in revenge, upon the shepherd leap ;
So, ruthlessly assailed and swept away,
Too oft, alas, he is himself a prey.
Thus, lately, did the ravening surge invade
The *China's* bridge, there deadly havoc made.
From their bleak post her faithful guardians hurled,
And o'er its prize in hideous triumph curled.
Though, rudely nurtured on the boisterous main,
My hoarse gruff voice for soft elegiac strain
Is all unfit, yet would I here lament

The comrades from us thus untimely rent ;
For who so stern but must at least bemoan
A fate which any day may be his own. ·
No more uproused the weary watch to keep,
Beneath the wave how peacefully they sleep ;
And undisturbed, though howling tempests blow,
Enjoy a long unbroken watch below ;
Till the Great Captain's awful voice commands
The Angel of the Trump to pipe all hands !
The sea at that dread summons shall subside
And in Earth's inmost deep recesses hide,
Bare the hid treasures of its oozy bed,
And, *living*, loathly yield its hoarded dead.

Enough.   Why cram the dull prosaic page
With all the details of this wondrous age?
Since, once its coming great achievements done,
'Twill prove a brief and transitory one,
A flitting dawn to quell chaotic night
And usher in an Age of perfect Light.
As yet poor man, to his advantage blind,
The slave of habit, hath not tuned his mind
To such a key as with its spirit chimes,
But holds the duller pitch of ruder times.
Though Nature's powers like fabled genii stand
Ready to execute his least command

Who holds the Lamp of Science in his hand,
The clash of jarring interests and claims
So checks his progress and diverts his aims,
That whilst a happy few engross the spoil,
The many linger on in hopeless toil.
This only for a time.   Ere long he must
To his exalted sphere himself adjust.
The form erect, the high aspiring mind,
Were for no base mechanic task designed ;
But rather, as befits a godlike soul,
To think, to plan, to govern, to control.
Earth, long inherited, at last subdued,
Shall yield in plenty then our needful food ;
And with scant labour, but enough for health,
Bestow on all a modest share of wealth,
With leisure too, their higher tastes to please
In genial intercourse and studious ease ;
While liberal sciences, ingenuous arts,
So mend our manners, mollify our hearts,
That crime will disappear, grim warfare cease,
And all the world enjoy a lasting peace.

PART THE THIRD.

PART THE THIRD.

THE Blatant Beast, whose long adventurous quest
Had foiled of knights the bravest and the best,
At last, by courteous Calidore pursued,
Was by the elfin warrior's might subdued—
Subdued, not slain : no mortal arm could quell.
Save for a time, the loathsome spawn of hell ;–
But soon the muzzled monster broke his chain
And, rampant, ranged the troubled world again.
Though all have not the poet's piercing eyes
To know the demon through each quaint disguise,
Wherever foul detraction's voice is heard,
Or social mud by slanderous tongues is stirred.
The Blatant One doth nigh, in ambush, lurk,
And proves his hateful presence by his work.
When Israel in the wilderness repined,
And angrily its blameless Chief maligned :
When knaves stood forth, suborned by Ahab's wife,
To swear away the guiltless Naboth's life :

When hoary lechers, baffled, void of shame,
Traduced the chaste Susanna's spotless fame ;
In divers habits, various forms arrayed,
The Blatant One pursued his evil trade.

But why with trite examples swell the page ?
Amongst ourselves, in this enlightened age,
As gossip, critic, journalist, or sage,
Changing to suit the times his Protean mask,
He in new modes performs his ancient task.

Who but the Beast can edit or revise
That weekly foul miscellany of lies,
Mixed with half-truths, distorted, misapplied,
Unlettered souls the better to misguide,
Which rank and worth impartially defames ;
And, flinging filth at all illustrious names,
Out-libels so the Prynnes of former years,
One half regrets their pillories and shears ?

Who but himself, in less uncleanly dress,
Inspires that scurrilous issue of the press
Which, pandering to a vitiated taste,
Suffers no reeking scandal long to waste,
Unsniffed, its odorous sweetness on the air,
But stirs it up with most assiduous care ?

Have we not heard the Beast, bewigged and gowned,
In law (at least in impudence) profound,
Harangue our courts in most unseemly style,
And from the bar the judge himself revile?

Have we not seen, and almost wept to see,
(Calumniating Fiend! possessed by thee)
A restless politician, out of place,
His well-earned fame most piteously efface;
And clamorously from cold oblivion's shelf
Malign his rivals, glorify himself?
Why couldst thou not, O hell-born monster, stay
Thy greedy stomach with some meaner prey?
Why not in thy pernicious cause engage
Some acid spinster of uncertain age?
Some tattling seamstress, say, to whom belong
The piercing needle and more piercing tongue;
Who, in one shake of her malicious head,
Can smirch a character and wax a thread;
And on her task intent, and eke her theme,
Impale at once a maiden and a seam.

Since thus the Blatant Monster roams the earth
To mangle merit and disparage worth,
Shalt thou escape, incomparable *Weed*,
That dost all other plants in worth exceed?

Shalt thou escape, that dost so far surpass
Each fragrant blossom and nutritious grass,
That flower and fruit, with everything that grows
To please man's palate or regale his nose,
Whose juices nourish, or whose beauties charm,
Award with one accord to thee the palm ;
And crowned with varied blooms, bedight with green,
Bow to thy worth and hail thee as their queen.

The homely sage, to cooks and housewives dear,
In stuffing prized, and deemed without a peer,
Since, were its appetising aid unsought,
Duck were insipid, sucking porket nought :
Mint too, without whose sauce the tender lamb
Were torn in vain, untimely, from its dam :
Leek, onion, parsley, and sweet-smelling thyme ;
Nor these alone, of savoury herbs the prime,
But meaner ones in kitchen gardens grown,
Of names and properties to me unknown,
Right heartily, without a jealous qualm,
Award with one accord to thee the palm ;
Veil their own worth in humbleness of mien,
But bow to thine, and hail thee as their queen.

The flaunting peony, the primrose pale,
The hardy wall-flower and the jasmine frail,

The floral hauntress of the murmuring brook,
The lowly sweet one of the sheltered nook,
The velvet-petalled pansy, tulip gay,
The wee forget-me-not, the scented may,
The golden buttercup, the daisy pied,
Sweet-william, gilly-flower and London pride,
The stainless lily and the blushing rose ;
Yea, every flower that in the garden blows,
And all the exotic greenhouse-pampered tribe
I scarce could name and not at all describe,
With all that bloom on woodland, heath, or farm,
Award with one accord to thee the palm ;
Diffuse their odours, don their brightest sheen,
But bow to thee, and hail thee as their queen.

Man's blithesome friend, the cluster-bearing vine,
Whose blood, fermented, turns to generous wine—
Distilled, to draughts of wild delirious joy
Which gladden, madden, quicken and destroy :
The jocund barley-corn, whose potent brew,
Meat, drink, in one, doth cheer and strengthen too .
The toothsome cane whose rich substantial juice
Supplies the grog for hardy sailors' use :
The purple-berried shrub, by rustics prized,
Whose liquor, mulled, is not to be despised :
The bush whence frugal dames a fluid gain

That rivals, save in price, the best Champagne ;
With all that flavour drinks, man's thirst to slake,
Or temper water for his stomach's sake,
Which bless the user, the abuser harm,
Award with one accord to thee the palm ;
And send their choicest to the festive scene,
A willing tribute to their honoured queen.

All plants remedial, all wholesome trees
Of mystic power to combat dire disease,
Which, given by nature to alleviate pain,
The vexed physician's doubtful art sustain ;
As rhubarb, senna, castor, camomile,
Which purge gross humours and correct the bile ;
The famed Peruvian stem whose bark alone
Recruits the fevered sufferer's shattered tone ;
The Lethean flower whose soporific juice
Can sleep or blank forgetfulness induce ;
And (being for the body's use assigned,
Whilst thou alone canst soothe the harassed mind),
All plants which yield or balsam, drug or balm,
Award with one accord to thee the palm ;
All, crowned with varied blooms, bedight with green,
Bow to thy worth, and hail thee as their queen.

Well might the Blatant Monster's wrath be stirred

To-see *the Weed* so honoured and preferred ;
And since he could no fitting agent find
To wreak his spite, he presently designed,
Of base materials compact with skill,
An instrument to work his wicked will.
A heap of prejudice, a grain of sense,
A little knowledge with a huge pretence,
A mule-like stubbornness, a rancorous hate
Which no forbearance may at all abate,
Vile envy too, which rather would destroy
Another's happiness than share his joy ;
All these he mixed, and in a frame confined
(A fit receptacle for such a mind),
With brazen front endowed, a heart of stone,
And impudence unblushing as his own ;
But to the wretch a qualmish stomach gave,
Who (should he e'er the sweet indulgence crave)
Must from Nicotia's tranquil joys abstain,
Or them atone with vomiting and pain.

By this vile thing, the anti-smoker named,
The Weed hath long been libelled and defamed :
But though his wanton falsehoods well provoke
Invective keen and sharp satiric stroke,
The callous offspring of the Blatant Beast
Can both endure, nor suffer in the least.

Shielded with infamy, no railing tongue,
Not calumny itself can do him wrong :
As well attempt to foul a miry ditch,
To soil a dung-heap, or to blacken pitch.
But you, by wiles delusive led astray,
Who blindly follow where he leads the way,
And with an honest though misguided zeal
Malign a pleasure you have yet to feel ;
Let Error's veil no more obstruct your sight,
Admit of long neglected Truth the light,
Now reason, clad in harsh and rugged lines
But reason still, athwart your darkness shines.

Go search the highway, skim the busy street,
And all impound you happen there to meet ;
The motley throng in parties twain divide ;
Pick out the smokers ; set them on one side.
Are those all healthy, strong, of fine physique—
These sickly, dull, degenerate, and weak ?
Are those all generous, learned, and refined,
Robust of body, and acute of mind,
Of sound morality, of cultured taste,—
These clownish, stupid, selfish, and debased ?
Or, foolish one, take up the scroll of Fame,
There note each honoured and illustrious name,
As well of men who hold the helm of State,

And tower in senates, giants of debate,
As of those peerless ones to whom belong
The highest honours of romance and song,
Of science, law, philosophy and art,—
Divide them. Count your anti-smoking part.

The Weed injurious! Whoso dares maintain
The gross assumption against facts so plain,
Must obstinately stand as far aloof
From observation and inductive proof
As did that frivolous and pedantic fool,
First of the sect and founder of the school,
Who (in his wild impeachment of the Weed,
And of the ills which from its use proceed)
Declares that from its odorous smoke remains
A sooty paste which clogs the user's brains ;
And that, upon dissection, we should find
His corporal tissues with pure carbon lined,—
Forgetting that the ebon shade within
Would surely stain the white transparent skin,
And thus the smoker, mellow, old and ripe,
Would change his tint and colour with his pipe !

But ' Hold !' I hear our adversary cry,
' On no such partial ground the issue try.

This baneful plant, alas, doth not debase
The individual merely, but the race.
Though from its fumes no present evil rise,
And long the subtle venom dormant lies,
Its tainted leaven in the system lurks,
Which imperceptibly but surely works
(By generation spread) in all mankind
Degeneracy of body and of mind.'

A bold conclusion, friend, but most unsound,
Since, were there such degeneracy found,
It might proceed from quite a different cause,
Some general breach of Nature's wholesome laws.
But needless here into the cause to pry,
The thing itself we utterly deny ;—
Nay, hope to prove in reasonable rhymes,
That with the man of ante-smoking times
The modern smoking Briton fairly vies
In intellect and courage, strength and size.
You doubt it, sceptic !　Go next Lord Mayor's day
To London : at its ancient Turret stay :
Borrow the armour.　Should its guardian frown.
The dwarf ! the manikin ! knock—blow him down.
Take what comes first, nor stop to pick the least,
Then visit with your spoil the civic feast.
Go boldly in—this verse your warrant be—

And arm the trencher-warriors cap-a-pie.
'Impossible! The iron suits are all'—
Shades of my giant sires! too big? ' *Too small !* '

Trite is his story who, with love elate,
Contemned the perils of the narrow strait,
By plunging feet upborne and spreading arms,
To force a passage to his Hero's charms.
For this great feat of undegenerate days
Scribes have recorded, poets sung his praise.
To us, enfeebled by three centuries' smoke,
To swim the Hellespont were but a joke ;
So many have Leander far excelled,
Who by no lover's frantic zeal impelled,
For exercise or sport have stemmed its flood,
And some for nothing but to show they could ;
While one, hight Webb, (O may my verse proclaim
To ages yet unborn his matchless fame),
Immortal Webb, the first of swimmers he,
To prove his strength and bottom, crossed the sea :
Did through the surge by rhythmic strokes advance,
And fairly swim from England into France !

But though of strength and stature unimpaired,
How worthless both, unless we also shared
The martial fire which in our fathers burned,

G 2

And oft the tide of doubtful battles turned,
As erst at Agincourt and Poictiers ;
For till the sun that sees our swords and spears
To ploughshares turned, and pruning hooks, shall rise,
Security alone in valour lies ;
And frail his tenure of each cherished right
Who courage lacks in its defence to fight.
But though no mortal race may here excel
Our hero sires, their sons have done as well.
Let him who doubts if this proud boast be true,
Inquire at Blenheim, ask at Waterloo.
Would ye the bulldog-like persistence meet
Which gnawed its way to victory through defeat,
Peruse the story of the dreadful fight
Which raged round Albuera's bloody height
Till thrice five hundred victors did remain,
The sole survivors of an army slain,
And loosed the tyrant grip that strangled Spain.
Remember too, that chill November morn
Whereon a handful, famished and forlorn,
(To whom his fierce assault alone revealed
The foe, his stealthy march by mists concealed)
Long, foot to foot opposed and hand to hand,
Maintained against a host their stubborn stand ;
Till, summoned by the trumpet's warning bray,
Half clad, half armed, their fellows joined the fray,

Triumphant strategy with valour foiled,
And with success their chief's neglect assoiled.

Again : what feat of chivalric emprize
In reckless daring Scarlett's charge outvies,
Whose hare-brained troopers, blundering on the foe,
Outnumbered twentyfold, disdained to show
Their backs in honourable and safe retreat ;
But through his ranks, as through a field of wheat
The whirlwind sweeps, resistless in its wrath,
Rode on and left like ruin in their path ;
Yet saw the splendour of their triumph fade,
Outshone in glory by the Light Brigade ;
What time three armies viewed with bated breath
Its headlong progress through the vale of Death.

'Tis but a word : Advance ! and on they go.
Their lives are idly squandered : that they know ;
But heard above the cannons' ceaseless boom,
The voice of Honour bids them to their doom.
Blasted by bursting shells, by death-shots ploughed,
On, on they ride, impassible and proud.
Obedient to the spur and loosened rein,
Their eager chargers scour the fatal plain.
But yawning breaches in their ranks appear,
And bubbling death-groans drown the wonted cheer.

Smote by the fiery hail, they fall and die.
Here, horse and man, dismembered, quivering, lie :
There, riderless, the wild bewildered steed
Swerves for an instant and resumes his speed.
Mown down like grass in swaths they strew the plain :
They die unconquered, but they die in vain !
No ! Not in vain ; for never hero's blood,
Poured out like water for his country's good,
Was shed in vain. Those bones at random strown,
Like dragon's teeth in fruitful furrows sown,
Will prove prolific. On some fateful day
When England's host, oppressed, shall stand at bay,
O'erwhelmed but not subdued ; or if dismayed,
Of tarnished honour, not of death, afraid,
Shout ' Balaklava and the Light Brigade ! '
That shout shall nerve each arm, shall fire each eye,
And victory, unhoped, attend the cry.

Then, false one, where pretendest thou to find
Tokens of our degeneracy ? In mind ?
And did the men of ante-smoking days
For our dim light enjoy a glorious blaze
Of intellect and genius ? Nay, friend, nay ;
The evidence all tends the other way.
Though Chaucer like a ' bright particular star '
Uprose and shed his kindly beams afar ;

Though on his setting, twinkling through the gloom,
Did lesser lights their little spheres illume,
Dulness and Ignorance did still maintain,
In spite of all, their gross and sluggish reign ;
Still sat securely on their leaden throne
Till Raleigh made, O Weed, thy virtues known.
But when thy stupefying fumes had spread
Throughout the land, and addled every head ;
When fools and sages, peers and common folk,
Had dulled their wits with thy besotting smoke ;
The drowsy sisters from their seats were hurled,
And genius, like a sun, lit up the world.
The rosy dawn doth first serenely shine
With changeful glow in Spenser's work divine,
Wherein such bright fantastic shapes we spy
As herald Phœbus in the eastern sky :
The god himself, in Shakspeare, doth display
The fuller radiance of the perfect day ;
Illumined by whose ray, translucent, clear,
Nature and man, with aspect just, appear.
' But what to me—'   Aye, what, thou soulless clod
That dost in one dull round ignobly plod,
To thee, that Spenser seized the Orphean lyre,
That Shakspeare filched from heaven Promethean fire ?
Or what to thee their long harmonious train,
Whose tuneful pipings swell the choral strain ?

Then turn to that less pure though lofty mind
Which oped the gates of Science to mankind.

Philosophers for ages spent their days
Pursuing knowledge through an endless maze
Of speculation, frivolous and vain,
And never could to certain Truth attain ;
Till, dulled and darkened by Nicotian smoke,
The sages from their ancient trammels broke,
By Bacon led : henceforth the humbly wise
From fact to fact by sure induction rise ;
Till one doth from a simmering kettle learn
What power is loosed when earth's black entrails burn :
Another doth from falling apples trace
The law which holds the planets poised in space.

Hadst thou, O Anti-smoker, learned in youth,
Like them, inductively to follow Truth,
Grown old, from baneful prejudices free,
Thou hadst not censured smoking ; nor I thee !
Nor wouldst thou then, to facts perversely blind,
Have deemed Tobacco hurtful to the mind ;
But owned, that as all grosser plants absorb
Material force from Phœbus' potent orb,
Whereof a superfluity is stored,
Solidified, in many a secret hoard,

Till brought to light, and by combustion freed,
It supplements our weakness : so *the Weed*,
Ethereal plant ! the *im*material part
Of Phœbus' beams absorbs, bright gleams of art.
Sparks of intelligence, which, freed by fire,
As fragrant fumes exhale ; and him inspire,
Of cultured mind for their reception fit,
With lofty thoughts and more than mortal wit.

But though I in no measured terms exalt
The 'soveraine Weed,' I fain would shun the fault
Of such as mar the subjects of their lays
(Worse than with stinted) with excessive praise :
For well I know, things excellent in use
Are harmful too, inverted by abuse ;
And thus, what Nature specially designed
To soothe and stimulate the busy mind,
Of jarring friction to allay the strife,
And lubricate the complex wheels of life,
By tender youth abused, whose giddy brain
Knows not life's cares nor manhood's anxious strain,
(Its virtue misapplied) becomes their bane :
Like rich manure on empty fallows thrown,
Whose fertilising strength on fields unsown,
Far worse than wasted, in luxuriance breeds
A tangled growth of twitch and noxious weeds.

Own then the Wisdom which so long delayed
The advent of our plant : the dearest aid
To mental toil were wholly thrown away
While the mind slept and matter bore the sway ;
But when this tyrant, vanquished, half resigned
His staff of empire to awaking mind ;
The time approaching fast when all should drink .
Rich draughts of knowledge, read, observe and think ;
When thews and sinews should no more sustain
Life's duties all, but share them with the brain ;
And progress be the universal aim—
The *Weed* was needed ; and behold, it came.

To you, misguided ones, a word is due,
Who with less rabid hate the pipe pursue ;
Yet deem that all who seek its joys to taste,
By their enjoyment, precious minutes waste.
Know ye the bow will bear a constant strain,
And, ever bent, its pristine force retain?
The man whom labour, unrelieved by play,
Will not involve in premature decay?
You own ('tis universally confessed)
He must have leisure, pleasure, ease, and rest ;
Then let him in his idle hours enjoy
A pleasure, unlike most, without alloy.
But thou whose sordid soul all sense hath lost

Of true economy, and grudg'st the cost
Of this most cheap indulgence, see around,
What far more costly luxuries abound ;
And if thou deem'st extravagance a sin,
With them, O inconsistent one, begin.
Censure the follies of the rich and great,
The pompous equipage, the glittering plate,
The gay apparel and the dainty fare :
These are thy proper game ; but spare, O spare
The one which rich and poor in common share,
Which will the meanest with the greatest bless,
Nor injure either save through gross excess.

Though mother Earth doles out with niggard hands
Such paltry gems as wealth alone commands,
Her teeming furrows plenteously produce
Her real treasures for our common use ;
Hence, with a bounty prodigal and free,
Enough for all, O Weed, she gives of thee.

Go ask the scion of a kingly race,
The nearest to the throne in rank and place,
The destined monarch of a vast domain
With empire wider than the subtlest brain
Of learned Greece ere dreamt of, Roman sword
Conquered, or Punic enterprise explored :

Of him inquire, whose lightest whim commands
The rich resources of remotest lands,
Brought without stint of labour or expense
With new delights to gratify the sense,
(Since these by frequent repetition pall)
Does not the *Weed* in worth outweigh them all?
The precious herb, whose sweet but tranquil joys
Not use abates nor iteration cloys ;
Yet, common to the dunghill as the throne,
Sheds not its sweets on kings and peers alone,
But takes from poverty its biting sting
And makes the beggar happy as the king.

O kings ! O beggars ! O all ye that share
With them dame Fortune's smiles and fostering care !
Ye seed of Adam, from his curse exempt,
Who neither delve nor spin, nor trade, nor tempt
The treacherous brine ; nor sweating swinck and toil,
But live on manna from an untilled soil ;
To you at least it is not given to know
The full delights which from tobacco flow.
You, brothers, you, of high or low degree,
Who toil with head or hand by land or sea,
Smoking in hard-earned intervals of rest,
Are only with their full enjoyment blest.

The veriest drudge of all, who serves the state
Ill paid and oft unthanked, who bears the weight
Of government, and onward boldly steers
The vessel politic midst taunts and jeers
Of envious foes, and doubts of timid friends ;
Yet holds his course and to the helm attends,
Whether the public voice, that fickle gale
Of rash propulsion, swells the bellying sail,
Or baffled by a nation's wavering mind,
His shivering canvas hugs the varying wind ;
Nor swerves for fulsome praise nor reckless blame,
But ever keeps in view one noble aim,
Though libelled, slandered, and misunderstood,
His country's glory and her children's good :
This master-slave hath little time to taste
The sweets of idleness, still less to waste
On pleasure's giddy round ; yet even he,
Thou cloud-girt nymph, may yield an hour to thee ;
May sometimes in thy chaste caresses find
Rest and enjoyment.
     Yet art thou as kind,
Impartial spirit, to the labouring swain
As to the harassed statesman.   Not in vain
Shall he perform thy genial rites, who now
Steers through the glebe the earth-inverting plough,
The whilst a docile team of sluggish pace

An even pathway in the furrow trace.
But wherefore does that rustic, passing nigh
On each successive round, with longing eye
Inspéct yon leafy gnomon ?   Roused too soon,
His eager appetite forestalls the noon.
But when the sun its southern verge hath passed,
Joyful he hies to break his six hours' fast ;
Quaffs from his bottle first the gurgling beer
(How sweet that gurgle ' to attuning ear ') ;
Then from his wallet takes the homely fare
His careful dame did overnight prepare.
Stale the brown loaf and fat the salted meat,
But hunger makes the greasy morsel sweet.
Thrice happy swain, with health and hunger blest,
The meanest viands have for thee a zest
No wealth can purchase.   Happy too, thy state,
Whom joy attends, and dearer joys await !
Not long he lingers o'er his frugal meal,
Scant is his leisure and he thence must steal
Some minutes for a smoke ; so fills his pipe,
A short black clay one, of the common type
(Wherewith content, poor Hodge hath small desire
For dainty meerschaum or substantial briar),
And lest the breeze its flickering flame should snatch,
With hollowed hands protects the lighted match.
The *Weed*, ignited, sparkles in the bowl,

The nymph descends, her presence cheers his soul ;
And to that toilworn face an air is lent
Of tranquil happiness and calm content.

Since thus alike the statesman and the swain,
Remotest links of the laborious chain,
Enjoy the pipe, so men of every grade
Between, whate'er their calling, craft or trade,
With equal zest Nicotian pleasures taste,
Whereof to sing were, sure, a reckless waste
Of rude iambics : let us then recite
One last great instance of their wondrous might.

See where yon hoary pauper feebly crawls
Forth from such shelter as the workhouse walls
Afford to age and indigence.   The dim
Bleared eye, spare shrunken frame, and palsied limb,
Are not the work of Time's unaided hand,
For dissipation there hath set its brand
And vice its seal.   Deep lines, by want and care
Engraven, mar his visage ; yet the air
Remains of one by Nature once endowed,
By Fortune too, above the vulgar crowd
Yet vain for him the precious gifts of both :
A life of sensuality and sloth,
A vicious, wild, improvident career

Have sent him in his age to languish here,
Aimless and hopeless, in despair to crave
The last asylum of a nameless grave.

   .

Though Happiness from him for aye hath fled,
Though Hope, tenacious Hope, itself is dead,
The *Weed* will still that wretched one befriend,
Still to his woe some mitigation lend,
Lighten his dark despair and lend a brief
(Though evanescent, oft renewed) relief.
As when the cheerful sun withdraws his light,
The gloomy horrors of the Polar night
Are brightened by the aurora's transient ray,
Which flickering shines and simulates the day.

LONDON : PRINTED BY
SPOTTISWOODE AND CO., NEW-STREET SQUARE
AND PARLIAMENT STREET